NANCY DREW
#3
AND THE CLUE CREW

Pony Problems

JOHNSON'S
PETTING ZOO
come pet our animals
and ride our pony

BY CAROLYN KEENE

ILLUSTRATED BY MACKY PAMINTUAN

Aladdin Paperbacks
New York London Toronto Sydney

☞ ALADDIN PAPERBACKS

An imprint of Simon & Schuster Children's Publishing Division

1230 Avenue of the Americas, New York, NY 10020

Text copyright © 2006 by Simon & Schuster, Inc.

Illustrations copyright © 2006 by Macky Pamintuan

All rights reserved, including the right of reproduction in whole or in part in any form.

ALADDIN PAPERBACKS, NANCY DREW AND THE CLUE CREW,

and colophon are trademarks of Simon & Schuster, Inc.

NANCY DREW is a registered trademark of Simon & Schuster, Inc.

Designed by Lisa Vega

The text of this book was set in ITC Stone Informal.

Manufactured in the United States of America

First Aladdin Paperbacks edition August 2006

10 9 8 7 6 5 4 3 2 1

Library of Congress Control Number 2005938146

ISBN-13: 978-1-4169-1815-8

ISBN-10: 1-4169-1815-9

CONTENTS

Pony Problems

CHAPTER ONE

Petting Ponies

"I can't believe you're having a turkey sandwich again today." Eight-year-old Nancy Drew shook her head at her best friend Bess. The two girls were sitting together at a long white table in the River Heights Elementary School cafeteria.

"I like turkey," Bess Marvin replied, slowly opening her brown bag and peeking in. "Hey!" Her blond hair swung into her face as she suddenly turned back to Nancy. "How'd you know I was having a turkey sandwich? My lunch bag was closed." Bess pushed her hair out of her eyes.

Just then, Nancy's other best friend, Georgia

Fayne, showed up. George was also Bess's cousin. Even though they were all in the same class, George had stopped to turn in an extra credit math assignment before coming to lunch.

George plopped down on the bench across from Nancy and Bess. She dropped her lunch box on the table. "Nancy probably just guessed," George said, pinning one brown eye on Bess. "I mean, you've had a turkey sandwich every day this week. Since it's Friday, it's easy to guess that you'd have it again today."

"Nancy never guesses," Bess reminded George. "She uses clues to figure stuff out." The girls turned to look at Nancy, who simply smiled.

"It doesn't take a detective to solve this mystery," Nancy remarked. "Bess is the only one I know who likes ketchup on her turkey sandwich." Pointing at the bottom of Bess's lunch bag, Nancy showed Bess the light red stain on the brown paper. "Your mom must have gotten a little ketchup on the bag when she was making your lunch."

Bess turned the bag to look. "I love ketchup so much. Maybe when I finish the sandwich, I'll eat the bag." The girls laughed.

Nancy winked. "The case of Bess's lunch is now closed," she said with a shrug.

"Not much of a mystery," George commented. "Wouldn't it be great if we had a real case to solve?"

Nancy Drew and her friends loved to solve mysteries. They called themselves the Clue Crew and had a detective headquarters in Nancy's bedroom. Working together, the girls had already solved a couple of good cases and were ready to jump into a new investigation. If only something interesting would happen . . .

"It would be fun to solve another mystery," Nancy agreed. She opened her own lunch box and took out some peanut butter crackers. "But it seems like it's going to be a quiet weekend.

Do you both want to come over tomorrow morning?" she asked her friends. "My dad said he'd take us to fly kites in the park, if you want."

"Sounds good," George said, before eating a spoonful of her yogurt. "Maybe I'll do an Internet search to check out which way the wind will be blowing in River Heights tomorrow." George liked computers and was always sharing interesting facts with her friends.

Bess rolled her eyes. "I bet I can find the same information on my new wireless radio. I built it from old parts I found in that junk shop on East Town Road. My mom took me there last week." Bess loved gadgets. Her hobby was building new stuff out of old pieces.

"It really doesn't matter which way the wind is blowing," Nancy cut in before the cousins began to argue over which was a better weather checker—the Internet or the radio. "Just bring your kites and be there at nine o'clock."

While they were having dessert, Bess asked, "Did you hear about the brown and white speckled pony Ms. Waters found in her garden yesterday?"

George's short brown hair bobbed up and down when she laughed. "My mom said she saw Ms. Waters running down the street in her nightgown, waving her arms and shouting about how the pony was eating her flowers."

"The whole idea cracks me up!" Bess exclaimed. "I mean, she's the librarian. She's always saying 'shhh' and telling us to be quiet. It's hard to imagine her running down the street screaming. My ribs hurt from laughing every time I think about it."

"Ms. Waters sure does love her garden." Nancy giggled. She tucked a strand of her shoulder-length reddish hair behind her ear. "I heard that the day before yesterday, Mr. Geffington found the same pony standing outside the post office. It was eating a bush," Nancy added. She took a sip of milk. "And before that, on Tuesday, the pony was discovered at the movies."

"Was it eating popcorn?" George snickered at

the thought of the pony having a snack.

"Nah," Bess put in. "It was munching leaves off that big sycamore tree in front of the theater."

"That's one hungry pony," George commented. "Does anyone know who it belongs to?" George's eyes lit up as she considered that there might be a mystery to solve.

"Buttons is Mr. Johnson's Shetland pony," a voice said from behind Nancy. The girls turned to see Stacy Quinn headed their way. Stacy was in Mrs. Bailey's third-grade class at River Heights Elementary. Stacy's long brown hair swung as she walked. "I couldn't help but overhear," Stacy continued as she sat down with the three friends at the lunch table. "You guys are talking pretty loudly."

Nancy grinned widely as a question popped into her head. "How do you know the pony's name?"

Stacy reached into the back pocket of her jeans and pulled out a picture. She handed it to Nancy. "See?" she said, pointing at herself in the photograph. "That's me standing next to Buttons." In the picture, Nancy saw Stacy wearing a T-shirt that said "Horse Crazy." She had her hair pulled back and tied with a floppy bow. Her arm was wrapped around a small pony. The pony was a little shorter than Stacy.

Nancy handed the picture to Bess as Stacy went on, "Ponies are amazing animals. I know all about them. But Shetland ponies are the best kind. When I heard there was one at the new petting zoo just outside town, I begged my mom to take me there. Shetland ponies are small. Even when they're grown up, they stay little. I *love* Shetland ponies."

Bess gave the photo to George so she could look at the pony. It had a flowing mane and a bushy tail. Stacy was holding an apple in the picture and smiling like she'd never been so happy in her life.

"All week I've been working as a volunteer at Johnson's Petting Zoo," Stacy shared. "Mr. Johnson lets me come after school. I brush Buttons's mane and feed him apples."

"Like in the picture?" George asked, handing the photo back to Stacy.

Stacy took the photo and said, "Yeah. Buttons always acts like he's hungry. Mr. Johnson only lets me give him one apple a day, but I bet he'd eat more. If Buttons was my pony, I'd give him all the apples he ever wanted." Sighing, Stacy put the photo back in her pocket.

"Buttons keeps escaping from the petting zoo. I think he's looking for food." She went on to explain, "There's an apple tree in my front yard, but Buttons hasn't found it yet. He's too busy eating other people's bushes and gardens. But someday soon, Buttons will discover my tree. When he does, I won't call Mr. Johnson to pick him up. I'll just keep Buttons. He's a great pony. I wish he was mine!" Then, without waiting for Nancy or the other girls to ask her any more questions, Stacy got up and walked away.

"Well, that was kind of strange," Bess said as Stacy left the cafeteria.

"Maybe—," George began, scrunching up her face as she thought.

"I know what you're thinking," Nancy interrupted, pointing her finger at George. "You think that the Clue Crew should investigate how Buttons is getting out of the petting zoo. And find out if Stacy has anything to do with it."

"You're such a good detective," George said with a laugh. "What was your first clue?"

"I didn't need any clues, because I was thinking the same thing." Nancy raised her eyebrows and smiled.

"Do you think we should ask Mr. Johnson if he wants us to investigate?" Bess questioned.

"We can start gathering clues and make a list of suspects," George suggested. "Once he hears the Clue Crew is on the case, he'll definitely want our help!"

"Let's get started." A faraway look clouded Nancy's eyes. "I suppose we should go to the petting zoo, but we're going to need a ride." She jumped up from the bench so suddenly she banged her knees on the bottom of the table. "I know!" Nancy cheered as she bent down to rub her sore knees. "Instead of flying kites in the park, I'll ask my dad to take us to Johnson's Petting Zoo tomorrow."

"That's a great idea," Bess said as she carefully

took the scraps of her turkey sandwich and tucked them back into her lunch bag.

"Aren't you going to throw away your trash?" George asked her cousin.

Bess grinned. "I was thinking that if Buttons is always hungry, maybe he'll like turkey with ketchup. I'm going to leave the rest of my sandwich outside tonight and see if Buttons comes to my house."

"You're goofy." George giggled. "But if there's a pony on your lawn in the morning, you'd better call me right away."

"Hmm," Nancy said thoughtfully, "I wonder where Buttons will pop up tomorrow."

ChaPTER TWO

Pony's Petunias

Saturday morning after breakfast, Nancy was getting dressed when she heard a strange sound outside her window. Looking out, she saw the cutest, shaggiest little pony standing on her front lawn! "It's Buttons!" she cried as she pulled her light blue T-shirt over her head and rushed down the stairs.

"Dad! Dad!" Nancy shouted from the front hall. "Come quick!" Her voice echoed down the long hallway.

Mr. Drew appeared from the kitchen, holding a cup of coffee in his hand. "What's the emergency, Nancy?" he asked, looking concerned.

Nancy's housekeeper, Hannah Gruen, peeked her head out from behind Mr. Drew. Hannah had lived with the Drew family since Nancy was only three years old. She cared for Nancy like she was her own daughter. "Are you bleeding?" Hannah held up a box of Band-Aids. "I was worried when I heard you scream."

Everyone knew that Nancy was a little clumsy. She had a bad habit of bumping into stuff and getting scratches and bruises.

"I'm fine," Nancy told Hannah. "And it's not exactly an emergency." She looked at her dad. "But it *is* exciting news!" Nancy opened the front door of their house so that the adults could see outside.

Buttons was on the grass, having a little snack from the flowerbed.

"My garden!" Hannah exclaimed. "That horse is eating my petunias!"

Nancy laughed. "He's

not a horse, Hannah. Buttons is a Shetland pony."

"Well, then," Hannah complained, "that Shetland pony is eating my petunias."

Nancy filled her dad and Hannah in on who owned Buttons and the pony's adventures around town.

Before Mr. Drew went inside to call Mr. Johnson, he warned Nancy not to touch the pony. "Just keep an eye on Buttons in case he walks away," Mr. Drew said. "Even though he seems like a nice pony, I don't want you to approach him. Let's let Mr. Johnson take care of Buttons."

"What about my flowers?" Hannah asked. "Buttons will eat them all!"

"Nancy will help you plant some new petunias next week," Mr. Drew said. "Let's get Buttons home safely first and worry about the flowers later."

Nancy was sitting on her front porch watching Buttons eat a pink flower when Bess and George came up the sidewalk.

"Oh!" Nancy rushed over to keep the girls

from crossing on the grass. "With all the excitement, I forgot to call you," she apologized. "Buttons must not like ketchup. He chose Hannah's flowers over your sandwich," she told Bess. Nancy pointed to where Buttons was standing. The girls were careful to keep their distance as Mr. Drew had asked. They went up to the house and sat together on the porch.

"I bet Buttons would love ketchup if he tried it," Bess said with a shrug. "Maybe if we get a little, we can put some on that purple petunia and see—," she began, but George interrupted, saying, "Look, here comes Mr. Johnson now."

A white truck pulled up in front of the house. The truck was pulling a small pony trailer. Painted on the side of the trailer, in big, bold, yellow letters, were the words: JOHNSON'S PETTING ZOO. And beneath that in smaller green letters: COME PET OUR ANIMALS AND RIDE OUR PONY.

"DAD!" Nancy hollered at the top of her lungs. "Mr. Johnson's here!"

"You don't have to shout," Mr. Drew said as he came out of the house to greet Mr. Johnson. The owner of the petting zoo was a bear of a man. He looked about the same age as Mr. Drew, but Mr. Drew was tall and thin, with plenty of brown hair on his head. Mr. Johnson was round and balding. He wore a white shirt with blue jeans held up by bright blue suspenders. There was a red bandanna tied around his neck, and he wore a straw cowboy hat on his head.

The girls followed Mr. Drew out to the truck, curious to hear what Mr. Johnson would say.

"Thanks for calling me." Mr. Johnson shook hands with Mr. Drew. "That woman yesterday, when she found Buttons in her garden, she didn't call. She just chased him down the street in her nightgown while she banged two pans together. I finally found Buttons a few blocks away, near the pizza parlor, eating berries off a mulberry bush."

"Good thing the pizza parlor wasn't open yet," George remarked, remembering how Stacy had said that Buttons was always hungry.

"Crazy pony," Mr. Johnson muttered. Opening the trailer, he grabbed a long piece of lead rope out of a box. "Why won't you just stay in the zoo?" he asked the pony as he slipped the rope around Buttons's neck and tied a knot.

Buttons neighed in reply.

Mr. Johnson sighed. "All righty there," he said as he pulled Buttons away from the flowers. "That's enough snacking for today. You're supposed to eat healthy hay like the rest of the animals!" Mr. Johnson lowered a ramp on the trailer and pushed Buttons inside, closing the door behind the pony. He double-checked the lock on the trailer door, saying, "We can't have you escaping while I'm driving you home."

Once Buttons was ready to go, Mr. Johnson

came over to talk to Mr. Drew and the girls. "Sorry for the trouble this morning," he said, lowering his eyes. "I'll gladly pay for the damaged flowers if you'd like."

"Don't worry about the flowers," Mr. Drew said. "We're just glad that Buttons is going back to the petting zoo where he belongs."

"I wish I could keep him there," Mr. Johnson said. "No matter how many times I check the lock on the pen, he still escapes every night." Rubbing his forehead with his fingers, he added, "It's a mystery to me how that pony is getting out of the zoo."

George leaned over and whispered in Bess's ear. Then Bess whispered the same message in Nancy's. Nancy nodded.

"The Clue Crew would love to help you solve this mystery," Nancy told Mr. Johnson. "We can come to the petting zoo right now. Can't we, Dad?"

"I thought you girls wanted to spend the day at Bluff View Park," Mr. Drew said. Then he noticed that Bess and George weren't carrying anything in their hands. "I see." He nodded slightly. "You already knew about Buttons's escape act. You girls were thinking about solving this one, eh? I bet you were going to ask me to take you to the petting zoo today, weren't you?"

Nancy was surprised. "How'd you guess?" she asked.

"I might be only a lawyer, but I'm also the father of River Heights's greatest detective." Mr. Drew smiled. "I know a clue when I see one, and you girls don't have your kites with you."

"That's good detective work, Dad," Nancy replied.

Mr. Drew laughed, leaned over, and ruffled his daughter's hair. "I've learned a few things from you, Nancy Drew!" He turned to Mr. Johnson, saying, "If it's okay with you, I'll bring the girls to the petting zoo so they can investigate this mystery."

Mr. Johnson didn't even hesitate. He gave the girls a big smile and said, "You're hired!"

ChaPTeR ThRee

Nancy's Notebook

Even though it was Saturday morning, there weren't many people at the petting zoo. Nancy wondered why.

Before they'd left the house, she had run up to her bedroom to get her new purple notebook and matching purple pencil. They were a present from Bess and George on her last birthday. Purple was Nancy's favorite color, and solving mysteries was her favorite thing to do. The gift was perfect.

Opening the notebook, Nancy wrote, *How is Buttons getting out of the petting zoo?* On the next page, she made two columns. One for clues, and one for suspects.

Under suspects, she wrote down *Stacy Quinn*.

Stacy said that if Buttons came to her house, she'd keep him. She also said that Buttons loved apples, and she had an apple tree in her yard. Maybe Stacy was letting Buttons out, hoping he'd come over.

"Nancy, hurry up," Bess called from inside the animal pen. She and George were excited to pet the animals and had rushed ahead. "Come see the baby chicks. They are sooo cute."

Nancy closed her notebook, slipped it into her pocket, and headed toward her friends. She was still thinking about Stacy and Buttons and apple trees. In fact, Nancy was thinking so hard, she wandered off the cement path and tripped over a pretty big rock.

"Oof," Nancy grunted as she stumbled forward and fell to the ground.

"Are you okay?" Careful not to let any animals out, Bess opened the pen door, shut it behind her, then hurried over to Nancy.

"I'm fine," Nancy told Bess. Bess gave her a hand up. "Good thing my dad was over talking to Mr. Johnson. He's always telling me to watch where I'm walking. If Hannah was here, she'd be putting Band-Aids all over me, whether I needed them or not."

Nancy wiped the dirt off her pants. "I really can't help being clumsy. Sometimes I just start thinking and my feet turn left when they should stay straight. . . ." Her voice trailed off when she saw the huge animal pen in front of her.

Sure she'd looked up when Bess had called her name, but she had been so deep in thought she hadn't really noticed the bright red, white, and blue painted rails of the tall, split-rail fence.

"Wow!" Nancy exclaimed, taking it all in.

Moving closer, she discovered that the top of the fence was slightly higher than her head. There was chicken wire between the rails so no animal could slip out.

Roomy bunny cages stood along one fence wall. A separate area for the chickens had a little pond. Buttons was wandering around, hanging out with the goats and sheep.

There was also a large shady area with plenty of room where the bigger animals could go if it was too sunny or when it rained.

Nancy opened the large, swinging gate just enough for her and Bess to slip inside.

George rushed over. "Nancy, are you hurt? I saw you fall."

"Not a scratch," Nancy replied.

George was happy to hear that Nancy was fine and handed her a quarter. "I brought some coins from my allowance," she explained. "Do you want to buy some goat and sheep food?" There were a few food machines hanging on one side of the pen fence.

"Sure. Thanks." Nancy took the quarter and walked over to a goat and sheep food machine. Buttons was standing in front of the machine, bumping it with his nose and neighing.

Nancy hadn't been allowed to touch Buttons when he was on her lawn at home, but now that he was back at the petting zoo, Mr. Drew said it was okay.

Remembering that Mr. Johnson said Buttons should be eating hay, Nancy looked around for a bale. It wasn't far, so Nancy headed over to it. Buttons followed her. "I know you're hoping I'll feed you some goat food," Nancy told the pony. "Wouldn't you like some healthy hay instead?" Nancy took a handful of clean hay off the bale. "Here." She held her hand out for the pony. "This is for you."

Buttons stared at the hay, wiggled his nose at Nancy, and then walked away.

I don't think Buttons likes hay, Nancy said to herself. She quickly opened her notebook and wrote, *Buttons doesn't like hay* in the clue column.

Nancy decided she'd feed the goats later. Now that she had one clue, she was excited to search for more. Tucking the quarter into her pocket, Nancy went over to join Bess and George.

Bess and George were standing near the gate talking to Mr. Drew and Mr. Johnson. Mr. Drew was not an animal lover and was shooing away a goat, who was nibbling on the side of his shirt. The goat didn't want to leave Mr. Drew alone! Finally, Mr. Johnson got some goat pellets and threw them a distance away. The goat hustled off to have a snack.

"I bought the petting zoo a few weeks ago," Mr. Johnson explained. "Before that, I worked at a bank in Hailey Town." Nancy had been to Hailey Town before. It was about a twenty-minute drive south of River Heights.

"I didn't like working in a bank," Mr. Johnson went on. "I always dreamed about having my own petting zoo. When this old farm was for sale, I bought it and we moved out here. I purchased all the animals and built the fence myself." He pointed at the small red barn behind the zoo fence. "I built the barn, too."

Then Mr. Johnson pointed to a brick house with a nice porch and a swing set on the side. "The only thing I didn't build is our house. It came with the farm."

The goat came back and was bugging Mr. Drew for more food. Nancy handed her dad the quarter George had given her. Mr. Drew bought a little food and threw it into the center of the pen like he'd seen Mr. Johnson do. The goat ran after it.

"My wife and I love it here." Mr. Johnson looked around. "Business could be better, however. I think that if more people knew how great Buttons was, more kids would come to ride him and pet the other animals. Buttons is a Shetland pony, you see." Nancy, Bess, and George all nodded. They already knew that. "Shetlands are great. They have sweet personalities, love kids, and get along with all the other animals," Mr. Johnson finished.

Suddenly, a loud, grumpy sound came from the red barn behind the pen. It was a cross between a sigh and a snort.

"Do you have pigs at the zoo?" Bess asked Mr. Johnson.

The zoo owner wrinkled his forehead and raised his eyebrows. "No. Just the sheep, goats, bunnies, and chickens." He looked across toward the barn. "And one escaping pony."

"Are any animals in the barn?" George asked, staring in the direction where the sound came from.

"No, they're all out here," Mr. Johnson answered. "The barn is really just a storage shed. No animals are allowed in the barn. They all live in the pen."

Suddenly the barn door slammed shut. The angry noise made such a racket that all the animals stopped eating and looked up. Nancy,

George, and Bess looked up too. They saw a girl about their own age, with short, black, curly hair. The girl ran out of the barn toward Mr. Johnson's house.

"Who's that?" Nancy asked Mr. Johnson.

They watched the girl fly up the porch steps and disappear into the brick house. "That's my daughter, Amanda," Mr. Johnson answered with a long, unhappy sigh.

ChaPTER FOUR

Collecting Clues

"Amanda seems supermad about something," Bess whispered to George and Nancy. "Slamming the barn door and stomping off like that. I'd like to ask her about the escaping pony, but I don't think she'll want to talk to us right now."

"I think you're right," Nancy agreed. "Let's look around for some clues, and maybe we can ask Amanda about the pony later."

Nancy opened her notebook and showed Bess and George the pages she'd started.

"This is great!" George cheered after looking at the one clue and one suspect on Nancy's list. "Tomorrow we can come over to your house and

I'll copy everything we find into a computer file."

Bess wanted to go check out the padlock on the animal pen gate. The girls asked Mr. Johnson if he could show them exactly how he locked up every night.

"You girls sure do take this detective work seriously," he commented as he walked with them to the large hinged gate.

"Yes, we do, Mr. Johnson," Bess answered. "The Clue Crew is eager to solve this mystery for you."

"Well, then," he began, "every night I give the animals a new bale of hay. Then I count them before I shut the gate. Lately, I've been taking special care to check that Buttons is inside the pen. He always is." Mr. Johnson closed the gate and hooked a small latch. After that, he slipped a large padlock through a hole drilled in the latch. Then he secured the lock.

"Can I see the lock?" Bess asked, stepping forward.

"Be my guest," Mr. Johnson said as he moved aside.

Bess pulled at the lock. It was firmly closed. She tugged some more, but the lock wouldn't open. "Can I check out the key?" she asked Mr. Johnson. Bess took the key and opened the lock. She shut the lock tightly and handed the key back to Mr. Johnson. "Does anyone else have a key?"

"No," Mr. Johnson replied. "I have the only one." He unlocked the gate and put the key in his pocket. "I take the key home at night and hang it on a hook in the kitchen. Every morning I get the key off the hook to open the petting zoo for the day."

"Has the key ever been missing?" Nancy asked him.

"Never," he said with a shake of his head. "The key is always right where I put it."

"Hmm." Bess bit her bottom lip. "Nancy, will you write down in your notebook that the lock works and that the key hangs on a hook at night?" She paused, then said, "Maybe we need another column for stuff we should remember."

"Good idea." Nancy made a column and added the two facts. She also wrote a reminder to think about why there weren't very many people at the petting zoo on such a beautiful spring day. Then she closed her notebook.

"There must be more clues around here some-where." Bess quickly surveyed the pen and the animals but didn't immediately see anything out of place.

The three friends decided to split up and search around.

"Over here," George called after a few minutes. Bess and Nancy hurried to where George stood outside the fenced pen. Through the rails, she pointed at a bale of hay sitting near the fence. A goat was standing on top of the bale, eating. Yellowish-green strands of hay were hanging out of its mouth as it chewed.

"It's hay," Nancy said. "There's hay all over the ground. That's not a clue."

George pointed out that the bale of hay was half-eaten.

"I still don't understand what the clue is," Nancy prodded.

"Well," George said. "If Mr. Johnson puts a bale of hay inside the fence every night and the animals eat it, why is there so much hay outside the fence too?" She pointed at the ground nearby.

"You're right!" Nancy exclaimed. "It *is* a clue!" She bent low to the ground to examine the evidence. Even though they were standing outside the fence, there was hay all over. "Do you think the goats, sheep, and pony can spit this far?" Nancy asked, then took a few big steps to where the last scraps of hay were lying on the ground.

"These aren't *camels*," Bess remarked. When no one laughed, she explained, "Camels are known to be big spitters. I read it in a book at school."

George laughed. "I get it now. But are goats big spitters too?"

"I didn't read about that." Bess shrugged. "I can check on Monday when we get to school."

"Maybe Mr. Johnson simply dropped bits of hay when he carried the bale into the pen," Nancy suggested. "But we should write it down anyway." She opened her notebook and wrote in the clue column: *Hay outside the animal pen.*

Just as Nancy was closing the notebook, Bess asked, "Isn't that Amanda Johnson over there?" On the other side of the pen, they could see a girl in white painter's pants standing on a small ladder, leaning over the top rung of the fence.

"It sure is," Nancy answered. The girls decided to go talk to Amanda about the pony's disappearances. "Maybe she's seen something suspicious," Nancy said as they made their way around the pen.

Amanda was busy painting. She was smearing a new coat of red paint on the top rung of the animal pen fence.

"Hi," Nancy greeted Amanda. "We hear you're new to town. I'm Nancy Drew and these are my friends, Bess Marvin and George Fayne."

Amanda didn't get off the ladder. She didn't even look down at the girls. She just kept on painting.

"Welcome to River Heights," Bess said, reaching up and putting out her hand for Amanda to shake.

Amanda didn't shake Bess's hand. She kept painting.

George began to explain that they were investigating the mystery of Buttons's visits to town.

"She won't talk to you," a voice behind them

said. The girls turned to see Stacy standing behind them. "I've tried a thousand times. She won't talk to me either," she continued.

Nancy felt weird talking about Amanda in front of her, but since Amanda wouldn't say anything, Nancy asked Stacy, "Why won't she talk?"

Stacy gave Amanda a second to answer for herself, but Amanda simply dipped her brush in the red paint and silently swiped it along the fence.

"Mr. Johnson told me that Amanda doesn't talk to any kids in River Heights. Not here at the petting zoo and not at school, either."

"Is she sick?" George asked.

"Nah. She just doesn't talk. That's all. She's refused to say one word to any kids since the day she moved to River Heights. I guess she doesn't want any new friends." Stacy shrugged and pulled an apple out of her jacket pocket. "I still try every day." Stacy turned to Amanda and said, "Hi. Want to go feed Buttons with me?" She held out the apple so Amanda could see it.

When Amanda didn't answer, Stacy said, "We have the exact same conversation every single day. I ask her to join me and she doesn't answer. I keep hoping that one of these times, she's going to take the apple and come into the pen with me. Until then, I'm feeding Buttons on my own. I just love that pony!" She called, "See ya!" over her shoulder as she ran toward the pen.

When Stacy was gone, Nancy stepped closer to Amanda and said, "We'd like to be your friends." Bess and George nodded their heads, totally agreeing.

Amanda didn't answer. She turned her eyes away so that Nancy couldn't see them. Then, even though she hadn't finished the fence rail, Amanda put the lid on her paint, tucked her paintbrush into her overalls pocket, picked up the small ladder, and walked away without saying a single word.

CHAPTER FIVE

Painted Pony

The phone at Nancy's house rang early Sunday morning.

"Hello?" Nancy picked up the phone after Hannah told her the call was for her.

"Nancy?" It was George. "You'd better come over ASAP. You aren't going to believe who is standing on my front lawn!"

"Is it Bess?" Nancy was kidding. She knew right away it wasn't Bess. George never got this excited about her cousin.

"No, it's Buttons!" George thought Nancy was serious. She paused for a second as she thought about Nancy's question. "You were kidding, right? You knew it was Buttons." Nancy giggled and George laughed in return

"Gotcha!" Nancy said.

"I'm going to call Bess now," George said.

"Okay. I'm on my way!" Nancy hung up, grabbed her purple notebook and pencil, and hurried downstairs. She paused to get permission to go to George's. The very second her dad said it was okay, Nancy fled out the door and ran the three short blocks to George's house.

"Hi, Bess. Hi, George. Hi, Buttons," Nancy greeted the gang as she hurried up the front walkway. Bess and George were standing off to the side, watching the pony eat leaves off the Faynes' willow tree.

"What are you doing here?' Nancy asked Buttons. Buttons neighed and chewed off a few more leaves.

"I wish Buttons could tell us how he's getting out of the petting zoo," Nancy said. "It sure would make this an easy mystery to solve." Buttons neighed again as if he understood and was trying to tell.

Just then, Bess noticed a strange red marking

on one of Buttons's back hooves. She pointed it out to George and Nancy. They stepped in a little closer to get a better look.

"Girls!" Mrs. Fayne called from inside the house, through the kitchen window. "Stay back from that pony. I know he likes kids and is nice at the farm, but you need to be careful when Mr. Johnson isn't around. I've already called him. He's on his way."

"But Mom—," George began.

Mrs. Fayne didn't repeat herself. She just shot them a warning look.

"No really, Mom." George moved back from the pony and closer to the kitchen window. "We were checking Buttons's hoof. It looks like he's bleeding."

Mrs. Fayne came out of the house, drying her hands on a small towel. Slowly she approached the pony, talking softly and making a nice clicking sound with her tongue.

"I didn't know your mom knew about ponies," Nancy told George.

"She grew up on a farm in Ohio," George answered. "Sometimes she talks about how much she misses living on a farm."

Mrs. Fayne put a soothing hand on Buttons's side, being careful to stay in front of his hind hooves. She bent low to take a look.

"That's not blood," Mrs. Fayne remarked at last. "Hooves are hard and wouldn't bleed even if he did break one. There is no scratch on his

leg." She looked closer at the red mark. "That looks like paint."

The girls were surprised.

"Paint?" Bess cried. "Like the red paint Amanda Johnson was using yesterday!"

Nancy immediately pulled out her notebook and pencil. In the clue column, she wrote down: *Red paint on Buttons's hoof.*

"Maybe Amanda got paint on the ground and Buttons stepped in it?" George asked.

"I don't think so," Bess replied. "Amanda was outside the fence painting. Buttons was inside with the other animals."

"Weird." Nancy tapped her temple with the pencil eraser. Since Mrs. Fayne knew about ponies, Nancy asked her, "Can Shetland ponies jump?"

"Do you think Buttons might have jumped over the petting zoo fence?" Bess cut in. "Maybe he dragged his hoof on the rail at the last second?"

"I was just thinking." Nancy shrugged.

"Jumping would explain the paint. And possibly solve the mystery."

Mrs. Fayne gave Buttons a final pat on the back and stepped away. "We didn't have Shetlands on our farm in Ohio." She came over to where the girls were standing. "I don't know how high Shetlands can jump. They're different from other ponies." A truck engine vroomed as it turned onto George's street. "Here comes Mr. Johnson. Why don't you ask him?"

Mr. Johnson parked the truck and pony trailer in front of George's house. The girls waited for him to get his rope and tie it around Buttons's neck. Before he put the pony in the trailer, Nancy showed him the paint marking on Buttons's hoof.

"Can Shetland ponies jump?" George asked.

"They can," Mr. Johnson answered. For a second, Nancy thought they'd solved the mystery. "But that's why I built the extra-tall fence around the animal pen." Nancy recalled noticing that the fence was above her head. "Shetland ponies can't jump that high," Mr. Johnson said. "Nope. There's no way Buttons jumped over that fence."

The zoo owner put Buttons in the trailer for the ride back to the petting zoo. "Why don't you come back to the petting zoo again today? We're open all day on Sundays, and I have a reporter from the newspaper coming. You can tell her about the Clue Crew and how you are working to solve this mystery."

Mrs. Fayne agreed to take the girls back to the petting zoo as long as she could take George's two-year-old brother Scott along.

"The petting zoo's the perfect place to bring Scott," Mr. Johnson told her. "He's going to love it. And because of the trouble Buttons caused this morning, I'll give him a ride on the pony for free."

"Your brother is a nut," Nancy said to George. George laughed.

Little Scott was riding Buttons, clapping his

hands, totally excited to be on the back of the pony. Mrs. Fayne kept telling him to hold on, and Mr. Johnson repeatedly showed him how to hold on to the pony's long mane. They had gone outside the animal pen and were walking around a small track Mr. Johnson had made just beyond the barn.

The reporter was there. She was taking pictures of Scott on the pony. Nancy had overheard

the reporter ask permission from Mrs. Fayne to take a few pictures for the article.

As soon as Scott's ride was over, Mr. Johnson came and introduced the girls to Sally Walton, the newspaper reporter. "Ms. Walton is going to write a nice long article," Mr. Johnson told them.

"That's right," Ms. Walton agreed. "Once I heard about Buttons and how he keeps escaping, well, I thought, this is a great story!"

She told them that the article would be a whole page with pictures.

"Isn't that terrific?" Mr. Johnson asked, full of excitement. "After people read the article, everyone will want to come see Buttons. He'll be a celebrity. Finally, people will fill up my petting zoo!"

Mr. Johnson told Ms. Walton all about the Clue Crew and how they were helping to solve the mystery.

"I need to talk to Mr. Johnson for a few minutes," Ms. Walton told them. "But will you girls hang around? If it's okay with your parents, I'd love to take some pictures of you for the paper and interview you for the article."

"You bet!" Bess, George, and Nancy said at the exact same time. Mrs. Walton told the girls that their parents would have to fill out permission slips to print their pictures in the newspaper. She handed the forms out and asked the girls to have their parents fax the forms back to her later in the day.

"No problem," Bess said, pocketing her form. George's mom could sign the paper now, since she had brought them to the petting zoo.

Nancy tucked her slip in her pocket too.

"While we're waiting," George suggested, "let's look for more clues."

They were searching around the animal pen for anything that seemed odd or out of place, when Bess stood up suddenly and slapped her hand against her thigh.

Hearing the noise, Nancy and George hurried over.

"Did you find a clue?" Nancy asked.

"No," Bess responded. "But I've been thinking, and I've decided something important." She paused. "Mr. Johnson is a suspect."

ChaPTeR Six

So Many Suspects

Nancy opened her notebook and asked, "What gives you that idea, Bess?"

"Well." Bess bit her lip as she thought. "What if Mr. Johnson is letting Buttons out on purpose? He said the petting zoo isn't doing enough business. I think maybe he let Buttons out so that he could call the newspaper and tell them Buttons is escaping." She nibbled her bottom lip. "I bet the newspaper wouldn't come to see a regular pony. Having an escaping pony could be a good thing for Mr. Johnson and the petting zoo."

Nancy turned to the page in her notebook where she had written a reminder about how there weren't many people at the petting zoo.

She looked around. It was a sunny Sunday and there still weren't very many people visiting.

"I think Bess might be right," Nancy said at last. She wrote Mr. Johnson's name on the suspect list. "Mr. Johnson has the key to the pen's gate. He could be letting Buttons out on purpose."

George scratched her head. "I'm not so sure. I don't think he likes Buttons roaming around town by himself. It's not safe. Plus, he asked us to help him solve the mystery. Suspects usually don't ask for help."

"Good point," Nancy agreed. "But I think we'd better keep him on the suspect list until we're sure."

"Hey, check it out." Bess suddenly pointed off in the distance. "There's Amanda Johnson." Amanda was over at the pen fence, painting the blue rail this time. "Should we try to talk to her again?"

"Let's ask her if she knows about the red paint on Buttons's hoof," George suggested.

When they reached Amanda, she was finished

painting the rail. There was a smudge of blue paint on her nose.

"Please talk to us," Nancy said. "We want to be your friends."

Amanda didn't say anything. She just gathered up her stuff and headed to the barn.

Not willing to give up, the girls walked with her and waited silently while Amanda put her painting supplies away.

As Amanda shut the barn door, George said, "Wouldn't you like to have some friends in River Heights?"

"No." Amanda put her hands on her hips. "I don't want any friends in River Heights." She looked seriously at Nancy, Bess, and George. "I have friends in Hailey Town. I don't like it here. I want to go back there."

"You can talk!" Bess said, surprised. "Oops, I didn't mean to get so excited." She stepped closer to Amanda and said in a soft voice, "I bet if you tried harder you might like River Heights. It's a really nice place."

Tears welled up in Amanda's eyes. She backed away from Bess. "I'll never like it here. No matter what! I never had to paint the fence as a chore in Hailey Town!" She wiped her tears on the back of her hand. "If Buttons would just go away and stay away, no one would come to the petting zoo. Dad would have to sell the farm and we could go back home." And before the girls could say anything to make Amanda feel better, she took off running toward the house.

The girls decided not to follow.

"This isn't going so well," George told Nancy and Bess.

"She doesn't want to be our friend, and we forgot to ask her about the red paint." Bess frowned.

Nancy took a breath and let it out slowly. "Can we be friends with a suspect?" she asked at last.

George squinted curiously at Nancy. "Why is she a suspect?"

Nancy took out her purple notebook and

flipped through the pages. When she found the suspects column, she answered, "Amanda wishes Buttons would go away forever. She knows how important Buttons is to the petting zoo. Maybe she thinks they can move back to Hailey Town if he disappears."

"You think she's letting Buttons out, hoping he'll never come back?" Bess was shocked. "Amanda doesn't seem that mean."

Nancy shrugged. "Maybe she just *really* wants to move back to Hailey Town."

"Amanda could easily get the key to the animal pen off the hook," George added.

Nancy let her eyes drift toward the house. She could now see Amanda on the front porch steps at her house. "I can't believe we already have three suspects. We're getting really close to solving this mystery!"

ChAPTER SEVEN

New News

Ms. Walton called the girls together just inside the petting zoo gate. "I have a few questions to ask you," she said. "When did you decide to investigate this mystery?"

Nancy had begun to answer when George's brother Scott ran past. He was chasing a sheep, which was doing its best to run away. Scott and the sheep went around Nancy twice. Then Scott took a shortcut—right between Nancy's legs!

"Oof," Nancy grunted as she stumbled backward in surprise. George caught her just before she hit the ground.

"Sorry," George apologized for her brother. "Scott can be such a maniac sometimes."

"It's okay," Nancy began, "I'm used to tripping, stumbling, bumping into stuff, and falling." She glanced over her shoulder at Scott. "Thanks for catching me, George." Nancy moved her legs closer together so there wasn't any room between them, in case Scott came running by again.

Out of the corner of her eye, George could see that Scott had given up on the sheep and was now chasing a goat. "Poor goat." George shook her head.

The girls laughed.

"Now then," Ms. Walton got back on track. "Tell me

how you heard about the pony popping up in town."

"Well," Bess began this time. "We all heard about Ms. Waters"—Bess began to giggle—"and how she ran down the street in her nightgown." Her eyes began to water, and she wrapped her arms around herself. She was trying to hold back her laughter. "She was chasing—" It was no use. Bess started laughing so hard, she snorted.

George took over the story. "Then, on Saturday, Buttons came to Nancy's house." George would have said more, but Scott hurried by. He was quacking like a duck and pretending to fly. "Mom!" George called to Mrs. Fayne. "Make him stop."

"He's just playing," Mrs. Fayne replied. "He's not hurting anyone."

"He almost hurt Nancy," George complained.

"But I'm okay," Nancy put in.

Mrs. Fayne went over to Scott and told him to calm down.

"I'm a duck," Scott replied. "I live at the zoo." He pointed at the pond and the birds.

"Those are chickens," George told him. "Not ducks."

"Quack," Scott said. "Quack. Quack." He was flapping his arms again. He climbed up on a bale of hay and leaped off. "Quack," he repeated as he landed in the soft hay on the petting zoo floor. He climbed back up to do it again. "Now I'm a goat," Scott announced, making a *maa* sound.

"Mom," George moaned, "he's still bugging us. We can't finish the interview if Scott keeps interrupting."

"Looks like he's busy now," Mrs. Fayne remarked as Scott struggled to climb back on top of the bale of hay. "I'll keep my little goat over here while you girls talk to Ms. Walton." This time, when Scott jumped, Mrs. Fayne caught him and swung him around. "Maa," she said to her son and set him back on the bale.

Ms. Walton asked the girls a few more questions about the pony. Then she asked them how the investigation was going.

"Pretty good," Nancy responded. She pulled out her purple notebook but didn't open it. "We have a few suspects and a whole bunch of clues."

"How are you going to solve this case?" Ms. Walton asked.

"Well," George answered, "we're going to head over to Nancy's house today. I need to input our notes into the computer. Then we'll work together to solve the mystery."

Just then, Stacy arrived with an apple for Buttons. "Hi," she said to the girls. "Who are you talking to?" Stacy looked at the reporter.

George introduced her to Ms. Walton.

Mr. Johnson walked over to them. "Let's take a picture for the paper!" he said. "It'll be great. After this, everyone will want to come and ride Buttons, the famous pony!"

Bess, George, and Nancy gathered together in the front row for the picture. Buttons was on the side, with Stacy holding his reins, of course. In the back were Mr. Johnson and a very unhappy Amanda, who had been forced to be in the photo.

"Smile," Ms. Walton said, looking though the camera lens.

"Fantastic," Bess grumbled. She leaned over and whispered to George and Nancy, "In tomorrow's newspaper there will be a photo of the Clue Crew standing with their three suspects!"

CHAPTER EIGHT

Cookies and Clues

It was Sunday afternoon. The girls were in Nancy's bedroom, talking while George booted up Nancy's computer.

"Detective work is fun," Bess said as she flopped backward onto Nancy's bed. The purple covers were crinkled beneath her. "But it's hard work, too." She grabbed a pillow and hugged it to her chest.

Nancy got out her purple notebook and flipped through the pages.

"Computer's ready," George announced. "I started a new file for this case."

"Great." Nancy looked down at what she'd written. "We have three suspects. Stacy Quinn,

Mr. Johnson, and Amanda Johnson."

From over at Nancy's desk, George stopped typing. "It's hard to think of them as suspects because we really like all of them. It's a bummer to think that one of them is letting Buttons out of the animal pen."

There was a knock on Nancy's door.

"Come in," Nancy called instead of answering the door herself.

"Hello, girls," Hannah said as she walked into the room, carrying a white plastic tray. "Why are you looking so sad?"

"We aren't sad," Nancy answered. "We just like all our suspects."

"Take a break," Hannah said as she set the tray on top of Nancy's dresser. "I made cookies. Eat. Drink some milk. Things aren't always what they seem. Did you review your clues?"

"Not yet," Nancy answered. "We were talking about the suspects first."

"After your snack, check your clues." Hannah walked to the door. "You girls know," she reminded them as she closed the door behind her, "that good detectives always think about their clues."

Each girl ate two chocolate cookies and drank a glass of milk. Full and happy, they were ready to get back to work.

"Clues," Nancy said, reading the column in her notebook. "Buttons doesn't like hay. There is a lot of hay outside the pen. Then, there's the red paint on Buttons's hoof."

Suddenly, Bess sat up on the bed. "I just realized something. Stacy can't be a suspect. The key to the lock is kept in Mr. Johnson's house. She doesn't have a way to open the gate."

"Good thinking," Nancy cheered. "I think we should go talk to Stacy again. Let's ask her if she's letting the pony out. That way we can cross her off our list for sure."

As a rule, the girls were only allowed to walk five blocks from Nancy's house. Luckily, Stacy lived three blocks away.

The girls were there a few minutes later.

George knocked. "Who's there?" Stacy asked through the closed door.

"Nancy Drew and the Clue Crew," Nancy replied. Stacy immediately opened the door.

"Hi." Nancy didn't waste any time. "Are you letting Buttons out at night? You said you would keep him if he showed up at you house."

"Sure, I'd love to keep him, but that's just a dream." Stacy laughed. "Buttons belongs to Mr. Johnson and has a good life at the petting zoo. I can visit there any time I want. Sure I wish Buttons lived at my house, but where would I put him? In the living room?"

"He'd probably enjoy staying in the kitchen," Bess put in, and all the girls chuckled.

Nancy thought of an important question that Stacy could easily answer. "Mrs. Fayne told us that Shetland ponies are different from other ponies. Why?"

Stacy didn't even pause to think about the answer. She quickly said, "In many ways Shetlands are more like goats than ponies." Just then, Stacy's mom called from upstairs. "I'd better go. We're leaving to visit my grandparents on the other side of town. I have to change into nicer clothes. See ya at school tomorrow."

Back in Nancy's bedroom, Bess suggested, "Let's cross her off the suspect list." Nancy got out her notebook and put a purple line though Stacy's name. George deleted her name from the computer file.

"Only two suspects left," George remarked. "If Stacy isn't letting Buttons go, who is?"

ChaPTeR NiNe

Thinking Thoughts

Monday morning the phone rang at Nancy's house. Nancy was already awake and ready for school, even though it wasn't time to leave yet. All night her brain had been working on the mystery. She hadn't slept very well.

Nancy was comparing ponies and goats. Buttons made a neighing sound, like a pony. He was short like a goat, but other than that, he looked like a pony. Goats ate anything. So did Buttons. Except hay. Buttons didn't like hay.

Her head was spinning from thinking so much.

When the phone rang, she decided that since she was up, she'd answer it.

"Hello, Drew residence," Nancy said politely, just like Hannah had taught her.

"Nancy?" It was Bess. "You aren't going to believe this!"

Nancy glanced at the clock. It was really early. "Should I guess? Because I bet I know why you're calling. There's a four-legged visitor at your house, right?"

"Yes!" Bess confirmed. "Buttons is eating our grass! Right now!"

"I wish I had time to come over," Nancy said. "It might be early, but Dad would never let me rush over there before school."

"George's mom said no too," Bess replied.

"Did you look around for clues?" Nancy asked. "Like when we found the paint on his hoof at George's."

"Of course," Bess said. Nancy could imagine Bess looking the pony over, searching for something unusual. "I didn't find anything. Mr. Johnson must have washed off that red paint mark. This morning, nothing looks suspicious."

"Hmmm," Nancy said, then went silent.

"Nancy?" Bess called into the phone. "Nancy? Are you still there? Talk to me. I can hear you breathing. Earth to Nancy."

Suddenly, Nancy snapped out of it. "I'm here. Sorry. I was thinking."

"Think later," Bess advised. "I'd better go. Mr. Johnson just arrived to pick Buttons up. I'll see you at school."

All day at school, Nancy was thinking about the mystery. She paid attention in class, but between classes and at lunch, she was constantly bumping into stuff, walking into walls, and tripping on the ends of her shoes. By the time recess came, Bess and George were afraid to leave her alone. She might hurt herself.

"Oof," Nancy said as she banged her elbow on the ladder leading up to the monkey bars.

"Okay," Bess told Nancy. "You'd better tell us what you're thinking, because school's almost over and we can't protect you forever."

"Why are you protecting me?" Nancy asked, rubbing her sore elbow. She hadn't noticed that Bess and George had been following her around all day.

"We have to save you from yourself!" George answered. "Your head is stuck at Johnson's Petting Zoo."

"That's not such a bad place to be stuck." Bess smiled. "It's superfun there. Did you see the article and photographs in today's newspaper?"

Just like Ms. Walton had said, there was a full-page article in the paper. Nancy had seen the picture of herself, Bess, and George with Stacy, Mr. Johnson, and Amanda. Next to that, there was also a smaller picture of Scott riding Buttons.

Bess grinned. "Remember yesterday when Scott was jumping off the hay pretending he was a duck? It was annoying at the time, but now it seems pretty funny."

"Quack," said George. "My brother can be such a spaz sometimes!"

"Maa," said Bess. "I'm a goat!" She held two fingers like horns on her head. "Maa."

"Quack, quack." George responded, flapping her arms and running in circles around Bess and Nancy.

"That's it!" Suddenly, Nancy's eyes grew wide. "Thanks to the both of you, I think I just figured out this mystery."

"What did we do?" George stopped quacking.

"How did we help?" Bess stopped bleating.

"What are you doing after school today?" Nancy asked Bess and George.

They didn't have any plans, except home-work.

"Good." Nancy seemed very happy. "Do your homework right away. I'm going to ask Hannah if she'll drive us over to the petting zoo."

"Aren't you going to fill us in?" Bess and George asked together.

"Later," Nancy said as the school bell rang. It was time to go back to class. "Meet me at my house at four o'clock. When we get to the petting zoo, I'll tell you the answer to the mystery."

CHAPTER TEN

Case Closed

When Nancy, Bess, and George arrived at the petting zoo, Stacy was already there. She was brushing Buttons's mane.

Amanda was there too. She was filling the water dishes in the bunny cages.

Nancy went to get Mr. Johnson. She told him she had something important to share.

"What is it?" Mr. Johnson asked. "Did you solve the mystery?"

Nancy smiled and said, "I won't tell until everyone is together."

They gathered inside the animal pen, under the shaded area.

"I know how Buttons is getting out," Nancy

began. "At first I thought maybe Stacy was letting him out, but then, Bess realized that Stacy couldn't possibly get the key to the gate."

George added, "We asked Stacy anyway. She said she didn't do it."

"Right!" Nancy punched the air. "But Stacy gave us a new clue."

"I did?" Stacy asked. "I didn't know I gave you a clue."

"You said something really important," Nancy told her. "You said that Shetlands are like goats." Stacy smiled. She was glad she'd been helpful, even if she didn't quite understand.

Nancy turned to Amanda. "We thought *you* might be letting Buttons out because if Buttons disappeared, you might get to move back to Hailey Town."

"I didn't let him out," Amanda said. "Really. I might not like it here, but I know how much my dad loves the farm. I'd never do anything to hurt him."

"Nancy," George looked surprised. "If Stacy

isn't letting Buttons out and Amanda isn't doing it either, there's only one suspect left."

"That's right," Nancy said confidently. "Mr. Johnson is letting Buttons out."

Mr. Johnson gasped. "No, I'm not!"

Nancy hurried to explain. "You aren't doing it on purpose." She looked over at Stacy. "Stacy, will you please tell Mr. Johnson the number one reason why Shetlands are like goats."

"Easy." Stacy folded her arms across her chest. "Shetland ponies can climb!"

"Oh my gosh!" Bess exclaimed. "Buttons has been climbing over the fence."

"Exactly," Nancy said as she walked over to the bale of hay near the fence. "Yesterday Scott climbed on the hay pretending to be a goat." Nancy stepped up on the bale. She swung one leg over the fence. "Stacy gave the final clue about Shetlands, and Bess and George reminded me about the first day we came to the petting zoo. There was a goat who had climbed on top of a bale of hay and was eating."

Nancy pulled herself over the fence, catching her back foot on the top rail as she leaped to the other side. For once, she didn't fall. She'd let her foot hit the fence rail on purpose, to prove a point.

"I get it." George clapped her hands. "The red paint was still wet when Buttons climbed

over the fence on his way to my house. Just like Nancy dragged her foot at the last minute, so did Buttons. He got paint on his hoof as he went over the fence."

"That explains the hay outside the fence, too," Bess added. "Buttons was kicking some of the hay over as he climbed out."

Nancy came around the petting zoo and back in the gate. "Mr. Johnson," she said, "I think Buttons doesn't like hay. If you want Buttons to quit running away, all you have to do is change the kind of food you give him." She paused, then added, "And when you put the hay in the pen for the sheep and goats at night, be sure to put it in the middle and not near the fence."

"Thanks," Mr. Johnson said. "You girls are good detectives." He immediately hurried over and dragged the half-eaten bale of hay to the center of the sheep and goat pen. "Do you think Buttons can climb out if I put it here?"

Nancy turned to Stacy. Stacy would know for sure.

"That looks like a good place," Stacy answered.

Mr. Johnson brushed a strand of loose hay from his hands, walked back under the shady area, then reached out and pulled his daughter in for a big hug. "I knew you were unhappy. I just didn't realize how bad it was," he told her. "Why didn't you tell me?"

Amanda simply shrugged.

"Well," Mr. Johnson said. "Now that I know, I think we should go to Hailey Town for a visit so you can see your old friends. Maybe we can go next week after school one day. Would you like that?"

Amanda nodded. "Thanks, Dad. I promise I'll try harder to make friends, and maybe then I'll like it better here in River Heights."

"We'd be happy to show you around," Bess chimed in. George and Nancy immediately invited Amanda to hang out on Saturday night. She agreed. They also asked Stacy. Stacy said she wanted to come too.

Plans made, Bess, George, and Nancy gave each other high fives.

"Case closed," Nancy declared.

As a thank-you for solving the mystery, Mr. Johnson invited Nancy, Bess, and George to the petting zoo the following Saturday.

Mr. Drew drove the girls there. When they arrived, the zoo was crowded. There were people in the pen feeding the goats, sheep, chickens, and bunnies. A long line went around the outside of the fence wall. Lots of kids were waiting for a chance to ride Buttons.

The second he saw the girls, Mr. Johnson came over. "That article in the newspaper really worked." He waved his hand around the zoo. "Just look at how many people are here to see Buttons." Mr. Johnson pointed

over his shoulder to where his truck was parked. He'd changed the painted words on the outside of Buttons's trailer. It now read: JOHNSON'S PETTING ZOO. And beneath that: COME MEET BUTTONS, THE AMAZING CLIMBING PONY!

In fact, Mr. Johnson had made a special show for Buttons to appear in. Every hour, he set out a bale of hay inside the animal pen, right next to the fence. People would gather to see Buttons climb on top of the bale and leap over the fence.

Amanda was always waiting on the other side to give Buttons a piece of apple or carrot or some of the new pony feed they'd bought. No more hay for Buttons!

After the two o'clock show, Nancy, Bess, and George rushed up to Amanda.

"Are we still on for tonight?" Nancy asked.

"A movie, then a sleepover?" Amanda looked excited. "You bet! My dad will drop me off at your house after the petting zoo closes."

"I picked the movie," George said proudly. "It's about a girl and her pet pony." She grinned. "Of course, this girl's pony can't climb. It talks instead."

Everyone laughed.

"Stacy went to visit her grandparents again today," Nancy told them. "She'll meet us at the movie theater, then stay for the sleepover."

"I can't wait!" Amanda said good-bye before she hurried off to tell her dad all of their plans.

As they walked back to the car, Mr. Drew put his arm around Nancy. "I'm so proud of you." He winked at Bess and George. "I'm proud of the Clue Crew, too."

"We made new friends," Bess cheered.

"And we learned about Shetland ponies," George added.

Nancy looked over her shoulder at Amanda standing with her father. "It's amazing how many people one escaping pony brought together," Nancy said. Then, smiling, she added, "This mystery is all 'buttoned' up!"

Your own little horse . . . of course!

Do you wish you could have a pony of your own? Well, with the help of the Clue Crew, now you can! Nancy, George, and Bess found a way to design their own little ponies, and the best part is, you can keep them in the house!

First . . . saddle up these materials:

2 corks (Make sure one is bigger than the other one.)

6 toothpicks

Black, brown, or yellow yarn (You'll need only a little bit.)

Black or brown felt (Black or brown paper is okay too!)

2 black beads or googly eyes (or a black marker)

glue (any type)

Now trot along to these instructions:

Stick one toothpick into the large end of the bigger cork. Angle the toothpick upward to form the horse's neck.

Stick another toothpick into the small end of the bigger cork. Angle this toothpick downward to form the tail.

Give the pony legs by sticking four toothpicks in the bottom of the bigger cork. Using glue, attach strips of yarn to the pony's neck and tail. (This yarn is going to be the pony's mane and tail!)

Stick the large end of the smaller cork onto the pony's toothpick neck. If you have googly eyes or beads for the pony's eyes, you can glue them onto the smaller cork. But don't worry if you don't have any materials for eyes . . . just do what Nancy does! Take a black marker and draw some beautiful black eyes on the pony! (You can even give your pony eyelashes if you want to!)

Glue two small triangles of brown or black felt or colored paper on your pony's head for ears. If you want to dress your pony up, you can cut small pieces of felt or paper into the shape of a saddle and glue it onto the pony's back.

Congratulations! You have just created your own personal pony! Don't forget to give it a name!